Public Library of
Johnston County and Smithfield
Smithfield, NC 27577

P9-ARV-777

BEAR ABOUT TOWN

Written by Stella Blackstone
Illustrated by Debbie Harter

WITHDRAWN

Barefoot Books

step inside a story

Bear goes to town every day.

He likes to
walk all the way.

On Monday,
he goes to the bakery.

**On Tuesday,
he goes for a swim.**

On Thursday, he visits the gym.

On Friday,
he goes to the toyshop.

On Saturday,
he strolls through the park.

**On Sunday,
he goes to the playground,**

SWING LANE
PLAYGROUND

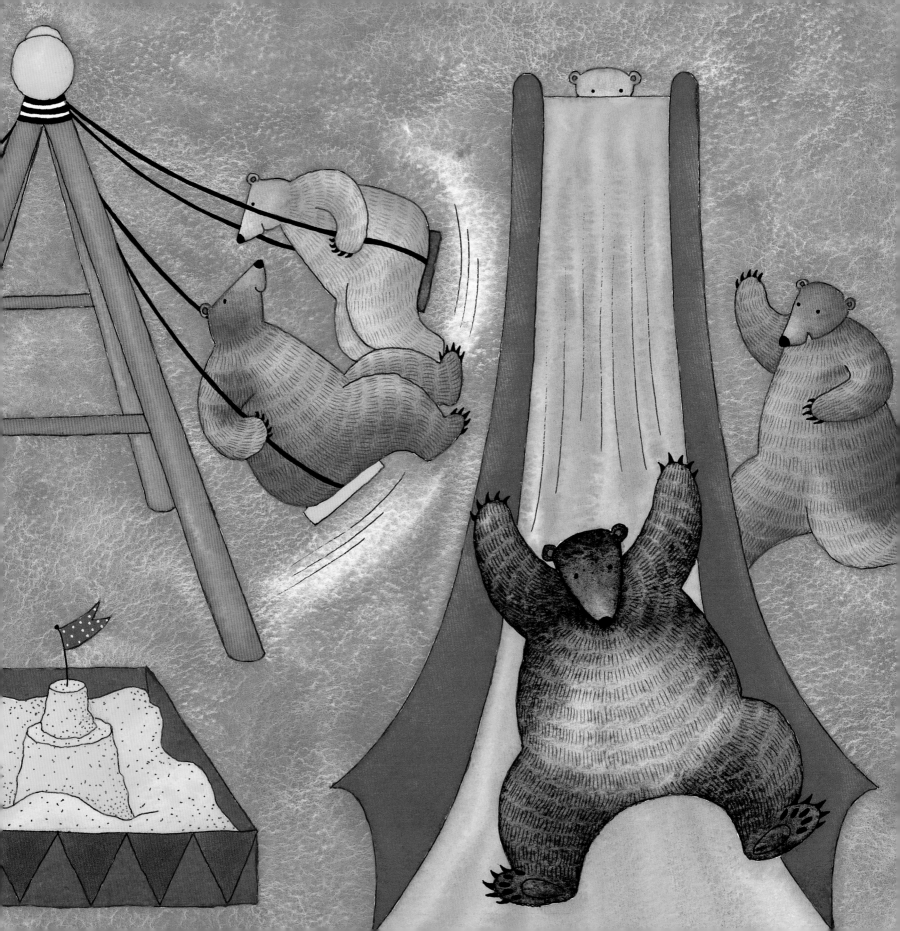

And plays with
his friends until dark.

Public Library of
Johnston County and Smithfield
Smithfield, NC 27577

WITHDRAWN

For more fun with Bear:

BEAR IN A SQUARE
Stella Blackstone
Debbie Harter

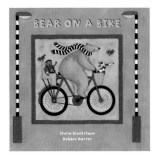
BEAR ON A BIKE
Stella Blackstone
Debbie Harter

BEAR'S BUSY FAMILY
Stella Blackstone
Debbie Harter

BEAR'S BIRTHDAY
Stella Blackstone
Debbie Harter

BEAR IN SUNSHINE
Stella Blackstone
Debbie Harter

BEAR AT HOME
Stella Blackstone
Debbie Harter

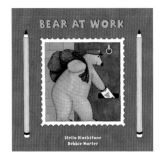
BEAR AT WORK
Stella Blackstone
Debbie Harter

BEAR TAKES A TRIP
Stella Blackstone
Debbie Harter

To Annabel and Dominic — S. B.
To Rosemary, John, Evelyn, Richard,
Rosie and Mary — D. H.

Barefoot Books, 294 Banbury Road, Oxford, OX2 7ED
Barefoot Books, 2067 Massachusetts Ave, Cambridge, MA 02140

Text copyright © 2000 by Stella Blackstone
Illustrations copyright © 2000 by Debbie Harter
The moral rights of Stella Blackstone and Debbie Harter have been asserted

First published in Great Britain by Barefoot Books, Ltd
and in the United States of America by Barefoot Books, Inc in 2000
The paperback edition first published in 2006
The board book edition first published in 2001
All rights reserved

Graphic design by Polka. Creation, Bath
Reproduction by Grafiscan, Verona
Printed in China on 100% acid-free paper

This book was typeset in Slappy and Futura
The illustrations were prepared in paint,
pen and ink, and crayon

Paperback ISBN 978-1-84686-027-0
Boardbook ISBN 978-1-84148-373-3

British Cataloguing-in-Publication Data:
a catalogue record for this book is available from the British Library
Library of Congress Cataloging-in-Publication Data
under LCCN 2005018208

20